UNDEAD PETS

FLIGHT OF THE BATTERED BUDGIE

For Mum – SH

For Amy and Sam the Man– SC

STRIPES PUBLISHING
An imprint of Little Tiger Press
1 The Coda Centre, 189 Munster Road,
London SW6 6AW

A paperback original
First published in Great Britain in 2013

Text copyright © Sam Hay, 2013
Illustrations copyright © Simon Cooper, 2013

ISBN: 978-1-84715-387-6

The right of Sam Hay and Simon Cooper to be identified as the author
and illustrator of this work respectively has been asserted by them in
accordance with the Copyright, Designs and Patents Act, 1988.

Printed and bound in the UK.
10 9 8 7 6 5 4 3 2 1

UNDEAD PETS

FLIGHT OF THE BATTERED BUDGIE

SAM HAY

ILLUSTRATED BY
SIMON COOPER

Stripes

The story so far...

Ten-year-old Joe Edmunds is desperate for a pet.

But his mum's allergies mean that he's got no chance.

Then his great-uncle Charlie gives him an ancient Egyptian amulet that he claims will grant Joe a single wish...

But instead of getting a pet, Joe becomes the Protector of Undead Pets. He is bound by the amulet to solve the problems of zombie pets so they can pass peacefully to the afterlife.

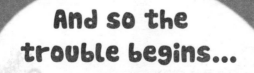

And so the trouble begins...

CHAPTER ONE

Joe grabbed a handful of strawberries and dropped them into the jug.

PLOP!

"Maybe a bit more banana," he said, stirring the mixture with a long wooden spoon.

His best mate, Matt, was standing next to him, bashing a bag of ice cubes with a rolling pin. He glanced at the jug. "There's no room."

"A few more blueberries, then…" Joe was just searching along the worktop for the bowl of berries when something hit his cheek.

UNDEAD PETS

"Hey!" He spun round to find the most annoying boy in the class, Spiker, smirking back at him. In his hand was the bowl of blueberries.

"Want some more?" Spiker fired another berry in Joe's direction.

He and Matt both ducked.

"Oi!" Leonie, who was behind Joe, let out a shriek as the blueberry bounced off her head.

Another volley followed. Joe and Matt dodged out of the way.

"Arghhhh!" squealed Leonie. She turned round to see who was throwing the fruit, just in time for a big squidgy berry to explode on her cheek. "Miss Bruce! Someone's splattering me with fruit!"

UNDEAD PETS

In a blink, Spiker slid the bowl of blueberries away from him along the worktop like a cowboy barman serving drinks in a saloon. "It was Joe!" he shouted.

"What? No, it wasn't!" Joe cried.

"Joe Edmunds!" shouted Miss Bruce from the other side of the classroom. "I'm surprised at you!"

"But I didn't do anything…"

"It was Spiker!" Matt added.

Miss Bruce held up her hand to silence them both. "Finish what you're doing, then bring your mixture over to the blender. It's your turn next."

It was Friday morning and Class Six were making fruit smoothies in their Design and Technology lesson. There was to be an official tasting at the end of the day by their headmaster, Mr Hill. The best smoothie would win a prize!

"Hold it still," said Matt as he poured the

bag of crushed ice into their mixture.

"What's your smoothie called?" asked Molly, peering over Joe's shoulder.

"Berry Blaster!" He scowled over at Spiker.

"Joe, Matt, hurry up!" called Miss Bruce, who was supervising the blender. "Bring your jug over here."

Matt shoved in the rest of the crushed ice and Joe picked it up.

Just then, something splattered on his hair. He spun round, expecting to find Spiker lobbing more fruit at him. But Spiker was over by the bin, fetching paper towels. Joe glanced around suspiciously. Who was it then?

SPLAT!

"Hey!" something else had landed on his head. Joe reached up and touched it. It was soft and squidgy. He inspected his fingers. "Urghh…" It was white with black bits in it. It looked horribly like bird poo.

UNDEAD PETS

There was a loud squawk and a brightly coloured bird flashed in front of him.

Joe gasped. He twisted round to see where it had gone. "Did you see that? It looked like a budgie!"

"Very funny!" said Matt, taking the jug out of Joe's hand. "And there's a UFO landing in the playground! Come on, or Leonie and Natalie will nab the blender before us!"

"Wait! Look over there!" said Joe. "On top of the whiteboard."

But Matt wasn't listening. He was already helping Miss Bruce tip their mixture into the blender. "Get the spoon," he called over to Joe. "There are some bits stuck at the bottom."

But Joe didn't move. He couldn't take his eyes off the bird. It was hopping along the top ledge of the whiteboard now, cocking its head and nervously looking around the room.

Joe blinked a few times. Why hadn't anyone

else noticed it? You couldn't miss it — bright green with a big scar and one bulging red eye!

"Must have got in through the window," muttered Joe to himself. Miss Bruce always had the windows open. She said fresh air was good for you. But Joe reckoned she just couldn't stand the smell of Spiker's sweaty feet!

"Look!" said Joe as Ava walked past with a bag of apples. "It's a budgie."

"What?" She glanced to where Joe was pointing, then rolled her eyes. "Very funny!"

"Hurry up, Joe!" Matt called from the blender.

"Hurry up, Joe!" echoed the bird in a high-pitched sing-song voice.

Joe grinned. It was mimicking Matt!

Then suddenly it fluttered over, landing on Joe's head.

"Hey!" Joe said, trying to swat it away.

"Hey!" it repeated. "Kissy, kissy!"

"Stop that!" Joe tried to wriggle free.

UNDEAD PETS

"Stop that!" copied the budgie. "Who's a pretty boy then?" it twittered, then dug its feet into Joe's scalp.

"Gerr-off!" Joe yelled.

Ava glanced up from the workbench and nudged her twin sister, Molly. They were looking at Joe as though he was nuts! Others were staring, too… Leonie giggled. Bethany pointed.

Joe was just about to shout to Miss Bruce, when the bird fluttered down from his head and hovered in front of his nose. It blinked a few times, then cocked its head at him.

"Sorry about that, Joe – just had one of my funny turns!"

"What?"

"My name's Buddy, and I need your help!"

CHAPTER TWO

Joe gazed into the budgie's single staring eye. "You're a zombie!" he whispered. That was all he needed! Another crazy undead pet – stuck in limbo land between this life and the next, until someone solved its problems. And thanks to a magical Egyptian amulet that his great-uncle Charlie had given him, that someone was Joe!

He sighed. It wasn't even as if he could ask the budgie what he wanted – not with everyone watching!

Just then, Matt turned on the blender…

SQUAWK!

The noise made Buddy shoot up in the air like a firework. He hit the ceiling, then flapped jerkily across the room before bumping into a pile of apples and crash-landing in the twins' smoothie mixture!

PLOP!

Thick green gloop splattered all over the worktop – and the girls!

"What was that?" yelled Molly.

"Yuk!" groaned Ava. Their shirts were covered in lumps of kiwi fruit.

Buddy bobbed up to the surface of their smoothie mixture, coughing and spluttering. He hauled himself over the edge of the jug…

SPLAT!

He landed on the worktop – a soggy ball of green goo.

Joe gulped. No one except him could see the undead pets – but they couldn't miss the mess they made.

"Was that you?" snapped Ava, glaring at Joe. "Did you chuck something in our jug?"

"What?" Joe could barely hear them over the noise of the blender.

"Was it a satsuma?" Molly yelled, peering into the mixture to see what had landed in there.

"I didn't chuck anything!" shouted Joe, just as the blender stopped. The room was suddenly silent. Everyone turned and stared at him.

Miss Bruce frowned. "What's going on?"

"Joe threw something in our smoothie!" wailed Ava. "Look at the mess!"

Spiker sniggered.

"I didn't!" said Joe. "Honestly, I'll show you." He picked up a wooden spoon and was about to use it to stir Molly and Ava's smoothie mixture, to prove there was nothing in there that shouldn't be, when his foot slipped on the splattered smoothie and he lost his balance. As he grabbed hold of the worktop to steady himself he knocked the twins' jug and it toppled off the bench…

A gigantic puddle of lumpy green gloop spread across the floor. For a second, no one spoke. And then…

"Our smoothie!" wailed Molly.

"Way to go, Joe!" yelled Spiker, who was jumping up and down with excitement.

Then suddenly the whole class was roaring with laughter.

SQUAWK!

Buddy took fright and flapped soggily back up to the top ledge of the whiteboard, where

UNDEAD PETS

he shook out his feathers and began twittering, "Time for tea! Good boy, Buddy! See a penny, pick it up. All day long you'll have good luck!"

Joe looked at Buddy, then at the sea of smoothie spreading across the floor. He wished the ground would swallow him up!

UNDEAD PETS

"Couldn't you have waited until after school?" grumbled Joe as he headed to the kitchens to borrow a mop and bucket.

"There's no time!" said Buddy, who had stopped twittering gibberish and was perched on Joe's shoulder, rocking back and forth like he needed a wee. "You've got to help me – now!"

"Why?" said Joe. "What's the rush?"

"My owner, Madge, is about to lose five hundred pounds!"

"What?"

"Her sister's going to steal it!"

Joe stopped. "Really? Her sister?"

Buddy nodded. "Unless we stop her, Madge will lose the money!"

"That's awful!" Joe thought for a moment. "Wait a minute! How do you know?"

"How do you know?" repeated Buddy.

"How do you know?"

Joe frowned. Buddy's mimicking was beginning to get a bit annoying!

Buddy cocked his head to one side. "Because I heard Madge's sister say so! They live together, you see."

"But why was the sister talking about it? That's not very clever."

They'd reached the door to the school kitchens. Joe could hear the dinner ladies clanking pots inside. "You'll have to tell me about it later — I've got to borrow a mop and bucket now, or I'll be in even more trouble with Miss Bruce…"

"Wait!" shrieked Buddy. "You don't understand."

"Later!" said Joe firmly, and he knocked loudly on the door.

"But Madge is in that kitchen!" cried Buddy. "And so is her sister!"

UNDEAD PETS

The kitchen door swung open and one of the dinner ladies appeared – red-faced and smelling of onions.

"Yes? What do you want?" she asked.

"That's her!" tweeted Buddy. "That's Madge, my owner!" Then he started whistling loudly and chirping, "Kissy, kissy! Buddy loves Madge, kissy, kissy!"

Joe gulped. It was Miss Pringle. Miss Madge Pringle. The Pringle sisters, Madge and Pauline, were dinner ladies at Joe's school. Although they were sisters, they were very different. Madge was loud and round with bright pink cheeks and wild curly grey hair that was always escaping from her hairnet. Pauline was smaller and spiky-looking. She never went anywhere without a thick smudge of bright red lipstick and a big squirt of stinky perfume.

"Yes? What is it?" boomed Madge again.

Joe gulped. "Er, Miss Bruce would like to borrow a mop and bucket, please."

"Pauline!" shouted Madge. "Fetch a mop and bucket. Beverley needs it in Class Six!"

Joe frowned. It was weird to hear Miss Bruce referred to as "Beverley"!

"Wait there!" said Madge, then she bustled back into the kitchen, half closing the door behind her.

"Do something, Joe!" cheeped Buddy. "Go in there and tell Madge what Pauline's planning!"

"Are you mad? I can't do that!"

Inside he could hear Pauline huffing and puffing, moaning about being too busy to fetch mops and buckets.

"They're always squabbling," sighed Buddy.

Just then the door opened and a mop was thrust under Joe's nose, closely followed by a heavy metal bucket.

"Bring them back when you're finished," said Pauline. And she banged the door shut.

"I still don't understand how Pauline could steal from her own sister," whispered Joe.

"They don't like each other!" explained Buddy. "They're so different."

"How?"

"Madge is a real saver. She loves a bargain…" Buddy seemed to drift off, daydreaming about Madge. "Two-for-one! Good deal, Buddy! Madge likes a bargain! Good—"

"Hey!" interrupted Joe.

"Look after the pennies, and the pounds will look after themselves!"

"Buddy!"

"What? Oh, yeah… What was I saying?"

"About Madge?"

"She's lovely! She liked to stay at home and play with me. She taught me to speak and sing songs and nursery rhymes. She loved my singing! Sometimes she'd give me a treat when I sang to her. *Round and round the garden, like a teddy bear. One step, two step, tickly under there!*"

"Buddy! Concentrate!" Joe said.

"Sorry!" Buddy squawked. "I miss Madge, that's all!"

"What about Pauline?" said Joe,

"What about Pauline?" mimicked Buddy. "What about Pauline!" Then he made a grumpy face. "She's always out! Shop, shop, shop! Naughty Pauline! Shops till she drops! She's never got any money – she spends it all. That's why she's about to steal Madge's prize! I tried to stop her, but I couldn't, and now look at me!"

Joe glanced up the corridor to check whether anyone was coming. He had to make sure no one heard him speaking to Buddy! "What do you mean?" he asked. "Did Pauline *kill* you? And what's this about a prize?"

"Well, it was last Saturday morning," began Buddy. "Madge was upstairs in the bath when a letter arrived for her. Pauline was going off shopping. She opened it by mistake – they've got the same surname, so it happens a lot."

Joe picked up the mop and bucket. "Go on, tell me the rest while we walk back to class."

The letter said Madge had won £500 in a department-store raffle...

I'll collect the raffle money and keep it for myself!

Pauline put the letter in her pocket.

Miss Pringle

I'll collect the raffle money and keep it for myself!

I like copying people. So I said it, too.

Pauline was scared Madge would hear me.
She made a grab for me...

SPLAT!

I tried to escape, but I didn't see the window.
I smashed straight into it!

Joe grimaced. "Is that why your flying is a bit wonky?"

Buddy nodded. Then he began to twitter again. *"Sing a song of sixpence, a pocket full of rye. Four-and-twenty blackbirds, baked in a pie!"*

"I think the bump's made your brain wonky, too," mumbled Joe. Then in a louder voice, he said, "So what happens now? What about the prize money? Doesn't Pauline have to go and collect it or something?"

Buddy stopped twittering. "Dunno."

They'd arrived outside the classroom, and Joe could see the rest of the class tidying up.

"Maybe Pauline's got the money already," said Joe. "Maybe you're too late."

Buddy cocked his head to one side. "No! I've been following her."

"What? Spying on her?"

Buddy nodded. "There's still time to stop

her! That's why I need your help — to get the letter back and give it to Madge!"

"What?" Joe gulped. "Steal it, you mean?"

"Yes, from Pauline's coat pocket!" Buddy nodded solemnly. "Her coat's in the school kitchen, Joe. You have to go and get it. It's the only way!"

CHAPTER THREE

While the rest of the class drew labels for their smoothie mixtures, Joe got on with cleaning up the big green puddle. He heaved another mop full of soapy water on to the classroom floor and sighed. He couldn't think how to help Buddy. And he really did want to help him – and Madge. After all, he knew what it was like to have an annoying sister. But there was no way he was going to steal a letter from someone's coat!

"You missed a bit," sneered Spiker, deliberately treading in the green gloop so he could spread it across the floor.

"Get lost!" Joe flicked the soapy mop at him.

Matt appeared holding a wad of paper towels. "Hey, our smoothie tastes ace, by the way," he said.

"Great!" Joe dunked the mop back in the bucket. "Maybe we'll win!" Then he spotted the twins in the corner, sticking labels on empty plastic bottles. "What about Ava and Molly?"

"They made another batch," said Matt. "With everyone's leftovers."

Joe watched the girls pour a jug of orangey brown liquid into one of the bottles. He felt bad that Buddy had ruined their smoothie. He glanced around the room. Where *was* Buddy anyway?

Then he heard a strange tapping sound and spotted the small budgie sitting next to the mirror above the sink, pecking it.

"Kissy, kissy," he chirped. "Kissy, kissy, for Buddy boy!"

Joe rolled his eyes. What a bird brain!

"Well done, Joe!" said Miss Bruce, who'd come over to inspect the floor. "You've done a good job. You'd better take the mop and bucket back now." She looked at her watch. "Be quick! The dinner ladies will be getting ready to serve up!" Miss Bruce turned to the rest of the class. "Everyone else, go and wash your hands."

Joe headed for the door, the dirty water in the bucket slopping over the sides.

"Wait for me!" squawked Buddy, swooping down to land on Joe's shoulder and gripping with his claws. Joe winced. He was beginning to feel like a pirate with a bothersome parrot stuck to his shoulder!

He headed down the corridor towards the kitchens just as the lunch bell rang and classroom doors sprang open.

"Watch it!" muttered a girl, as Joe bumped into her with the bucket, splashing dirty green water on her tights.

"Sorry," he said, doing his best to dodge through the crowds.

As they reached the kitchen door, Buddy pecked his ear. "Are you going to get the letter now? Pauline's coat's in there!"

"No! I've told you, I can't just steal it." He knocked loudly and after a few minutes, the door was flung open and Madge stood there, her face even redder than last time. She glanced at the mop. "Just shove it in the cupboard over there," she said, pointing to the back of the kitchen. Then she grabbed a tray of chips off the counter and bustled away, through the door to the dinner hall.

"Quick, Joe!" squawked Buddy. "Now's your chance!"

Joe hesitated. He'd never been in the kitchen before. It was strictly out of bounds to pupils. He glanced at the enormous steaming pots bubbling on the cooker rings, and the huge metal jugs of gravy lined up ready to be taken to the dinner hall.

"Don't just stand there!" said Madge, who'd reappeared. "You'll miss your lunch! Stick the mop in the cupboard!" Then she grabbed two gravy jugs and rushed off again.

"Come on, Joe! Pauline's coat's in the same cupboard!" Buddy took off, flying unevenly across the kitchen. "Over here!"

Joe followed nervously, dragging the mop and bucket with him.

Buddy was hovering in front of the cupboard. "Quick, Joe! Get the letter!"

With a slightly sweaty hand, Joe pulled

open the door. Inside were some brooms and, hanging up, two coats…

Joe gulped.

"That's Pauline's!" squawked Buddy, fluttering round a purple puffa jacket. "Look there! There's something in the pocket!"

Joe swallowed hard. This felt all wrong.

"Go on, Joe! What are you waiting for?"

But Joe couldn't do it. Even though the letter rightfully belonged to Madge, not Pauline, he still felt like a thief!

"Hurry!" trilled Buddy. "You've got to help Madge!"

Joe reached out and took the piece of paper. It was a letter from Beddows – the large department store in the centre of town.

B

Beddows

CONGRATULATIONS!

You are the winner of the grand prize in the Beddows raffle! Please bring your raffle ticket along to our store to collect your prize!
£500

Before Joe could read any more, he heard footsteps behind him. He jammed the letter back in Pauline's coat pocket and spun round. But he'd forgotten about the mop…

He tripped and stumbled, then lost his balance, landing bottom down in the bucket! Cold soapy green water seeped into his trousers.

"What's going on?"

Joe looked up into the shocked face of Pauline Pringle.

"What are you doing in here?" she demanded.

"Miss Bruce said I should bring back the mop and bucket. I knocked at the door and Miss Pringle – I mean, the other Miss Pringle – said I should put it in the cupboard. But then I sort of tripped over the mop and…"

Pauline rolled her eyes and pursed her bright red lips. "And got yourself stuck in the bucket!"

Joe struggled to his feet and the cold water dripped out of his trousers on to the floor.

"Mop it up," snapped Pauline, "then stick some newspaper down on the floor, so no one slips." She opened another metal cupboard and pulled out a couple of old newspapers and a box marked "lost property". "And you'd better borrow some dry clothes out of there!" Then she grabbed the rest of the gravy jugs and left him to it.

Joe groaned. That was the final straw. Now he'd have to spend the rest of the day wearing someone else's clothes. And even worse, the only thing he could find in the box that was his size was an old pair of grey tracksuit bottoms that smelled like someone had weed in them…

"What about the letter?" squawked Buddy. "You need to give it to Madge!"

"I can't!" hissed Joe. "In case you haven't noticed, I've got to clean up this mess!

And anyway, Pauline could pop back in here any time!"

He dunked the mop back into the bucket, gave it a swirl, then slopped it down on to the floor.

A few minutes later Pauline reappeared carrying a stack of empty metal trays that she banged down on the kitchen worktop. "That's enough mopping! Stick some newspaper down, then go and get your lunch."

Buddy was fluttering crossly round Joe's head. "Do something, Joe! We've got to get that letter! As soon as she's gone, have another go!"

But Pauline wasn't going anywhere. "I'll put it away!" she said, taking the mop out of Joe's hands and shoving it roughly into the cupboard. Then she turned to her coat, glancing furtively over her shoulder, took out the letter and stuffed it in her apron pocket.

"The letter!" shrieked Buddy. "She's taking

the letter away!"

"Get a move on," said Pauline as she passed Joe. "Or there'll be nothing left for your lunch!"

Buddy collapsed on the floor and buried his head under his wing. "We'll never get the letter now!" And then he started twittering again. *"Polly put the kettle on! Polly put the kettle on!"*

"Buddy!" said Joe, trying to get his attention.

But the budgie ignored him. "Kissy, kissy! Time for tea! *Happy Birthday to you, Happy Birthday to you!"*

"BUDDY!" said Joe. "Snap out of it!"

But Buddy didn't stop singing, and he began plucking out his green feathers, too. "She loves me, she loves me not. She loves me, she loves me not…"

"Stop it! You'll go bald!" Joe gritted his teeth and turned back to the wet floor.

As he lay down a sheet of newspaper, he spotted something – a large advert on the

UNDEAD PETS

back page. It was for Beddows Department Store, advertising a special one-day super sale on Sunday to celebrate the store's fiftieth anniversary. But that wasn't what caught Joe's eye. It was the line at the bottom of the advert that made him sit up straight.

> # GRAND PRIZE DRAW
> *The winner of our £500 raffle will be
> presented with their prize at 12 noon this
> Sunday. To celebrate, we'll be giving away
> a free slice of cake to all our customers.
> Everyone welcome!*

"Buddy!" Joe gasped. "It's Madge's prize!"

Buddy stopped gibbering and his head spun round to look at Joe, his beak full of feathers.

"Wmmmph?" he mumbled.

Joe frowned.

"Sorry," Buddy said, spitting out the feathers. "What did you say?"

"Look!" said Joe, pointing at the page. "It says here that the winner of the raffle will be presented with their prize on Sunday!"

Buddy cocked his head and looked blankly at Joe.

"Don't you see? That must be Madge's prize! She's supposed to collect it on Sunday. That means we've still got two days to find a way to stop Pauline!"

CHAPTER FOUR

"What kept you?" asked Ben as Joe came into the dining hall and flopped down in the seat next to Matt.

"Don't ask," Joe groaned. He glanced around. There were loads of empty places at the table as most of the kids had already finished lunch. Buddy was hopping about on the table pecking crumbs. Joe was glad to have a break from him!

Matt made a face. "What's that smell? Why are you wearing those?" He pointed at Joe's tracksuit bottoms.

UNDEAD PETS

"It's a long story," said Joe, stabbing a carrot with his fork and looking at his food miserably.

The carrot was mushy and the shrivelled slice of pizza didn't look too tasty either. He laid down his cutlery.

"You're not leaving that, I hope!" Madge Pringle loomed over him, a wet dishcloth in her hand. "That's good food, that is. You mustn't waste it!"

UNDEAD PETS

"It's cold," said Matt.

"And soggy," added Ben.

"Others would be glad of that meal," said Madge solemnly. "Now eat it up like a good boy!"

Joe tried to saw through the pizza crust.

"You need an axe," giggled Ben.

"More like a chainsaw!" sniggered Matt.

Madge gave them a stern look, then went off to wipe down a table nearby.

"So, what's with the clothes?" asked Matt.

"I had an accident with the bucket," mumbled Joe. He was still trying to chew the lump of concrete pizza.

"What sort of an accident?"

"I fell in the bucket."

Ben sniggered.

"Loser!" grinned Matt.

Joe used his finger to flick a small piece of pizza crust off his plate towards Matt.

"Hey!" Matt laughed. "Anyway, did I tell you I'm getting new footie boots on Sunday?"

"What?" Ben stopped eating his pudding and frowned. "You're always getting new stuff!"

"There's a big sale on—" began Matt.

"At Beddows department store?" chipped in Joe. "I heard about that."

"I wish my mum would buy me new boots," said Ben glumly.

"Tell her about the sale. There's free cake,

too!" said Matt. "I heard Mum telling my dad that he could go and eat cake while she went shopping!"

Suddenly a hand appeared in front of Joe and swiped his plate away.

"Had enough, have you?" It was Pauline. She was piling empty plates on to a trolley. She was about to scrape his pizza into a bucket of scraps when Madge thundered over.

"Stop! He's not finished!"

Pauline looked at the plate, then at Joe, then at the clock on the wall. "Yes, he has. He should be on to his pudding by now!"

Madge glared at her sister. "But look at all that good food going to waste!"

Pauline pursed her lips. "He was late in for lunch, so it's his own fault if there's no time to finish it. He's got to eat his pudding now!" She looked at the clock again.

Joe coughed. "Er, I'd had enough anyway."

The dinner ladies glared at him, then at each other.

Buddy fluttered over and landed on Joe's shoulder. "It's always like this!" he sighed. "Bicker, bicker, argue, argue. I wish they'd put a sock in it!" He shook his head and flew off.

"Give him his plate back!" growled Madge.

"No!" snapped Pauline.

Moments later, there was a loud bang on the other side of the dinner hall.

A large plastic water jug had fallen off the serving counter.

Madge gave a loud sigh, then turned to go and sort it out. As soon as she'd gone, Pauline made off with the trolley – and Joe's plate!

"Lucky escape!" grinned Matt.

"Yeah, I thought she was going to chain you in the kitchen until you'd finished it all!" giggled Ben.

Joe wolfed down his pudding, just in case Pauline came back. Then they trooped out of the dinner hall.

As they left, Buddy fluttered down and landed on his shoulder again. "Clever boy, Buddy! Buddy's a clever boy!" Then he leaned over and whispered in Joe's ear, "I knocked over the water jug to make them stop arguing!"

Joe smiled.

Buddy cocked his head to one side. "It was close to the edge – so I gave it a shove. Good boy, Buddy! Buddy is a clever boy!"

Perhaps Buddy wasn't as much of a bird brain as Joe had thought...

CHAPTER FIVE

"I still think we should have won!" grumbled Matt as he and Joe, and Joe's little brother, Toby, walked back from school.

"Won what?" asked Toby, who was walking along the edge of the kerb as though it was a tightrope.

"The smoothie competition!" said Matt. He and Joe had been talking about nothing else since they'd left school, but Toby hadn't been listening.

"Who won it?" asked Toby.

UNDEAD PETS

"The twins!" said Joe and Matt together.

"I think Mr Hill just felt sorry for them," said Matt. "Because they lost their first batch."

Joe glanced at Buddy out of the corner of his eye. The budgie was hopping up and down on his shoulder, whistling tunelessly.

"Want to come round to my house and play Xbox tonight?" asked Matt.

"I can't," said Joe. "I'm helping Mum with the leaflets for her new business."

"Eh?" Matt looked at him blankly.

"You know, my mum's new mobile hairdressing business."

Matt shrugged.

"She's left the hair salon and set up on her own. She's going to cut people's hair in their own homes."

"Oh, right," said Matt. "And you're going to be doing that all night?"

"Yeah, well, I said I'd help her sort out the

leaflets she's had printed. We're going to put them through people's letterboxes tomorrow to try and get her some customers."

"What?" Buddy stopped whistling and gave a squawk. "But you've got to go round to Madge's house tomorrow and find the letter!"

Joe ignored him. "She's paying me," he added. "Hey, do you want to help delivering them? I'll split the money with you."

Matt shrugged. "OK."

Buddy was shrieking now. "What about Madge? You need to get that letter!"

When Joe didn't reply, Buddy pecked his ear.

"Yow!" Joe tried to bat Buddy away, but he'd already taken off — fluttering lopsidedly up into the branches of a nearby tree, where he sat twittering angrily.

Joe rubbed his ear.

"What happened?" Matt asked.

"Wow!" said Toby, his eyes like saucers. "Your ear's bright red!"

"Er, something must have stung me," Joe mumbled.

"What? Like a killer bee?" Toby was peering at his ear now. "I saw some on TV! They stung a man's nose and it swelled up, then exploded!"

"Great!" Joe rolled his eyes. "Come on, Toby. Mum will be waiting…"

"Why did you nip me?" Joe asked.

Buddy was sitting on top of the curtain pole in Joe's bedroom, his head tucked under his wing, muttering to himself. "Bad Buddy. Buddy is a bad, bad, boy!"

Joe groaned. "Don't go all bonkers on me again!"

Buddy shook his feathers. "Sorry! Sorry about pecking you… But I hate it when people ignore me!" He puffed up his little chest and let out a deep sigh. "What's the plan to stop Pauline?"

Joe sank down on to his bed. "Dunno." He glanced aimlessly round the room. Then his eyes rested on the magical Egyptian amulet Uncle Charlie had given him. It was small and black and shaped like a jackal. It was this amulet that had started all of his undead pet troubles in the first place!

Joe reached over to pick it up, and spotted something underneath.

UNDEAD PETS

"Raffle tickets!"

Buddy flew over to Joe.

"Look," said Joe. "These are raffle tickets I got from the football club. I've got to keep them safe until the draw."

Buddy shrugged. He still looked like his brain had gone on holiday.

"When I bought these tickets," explained Joe, "the football club kept one half of the ticket — the stubby bit. And they gave me the other half, see?" Joe showed Buddy the tear down the side of the tickets. "The bit the footie club keeps goes in a hat and when they've sold all the tickets they pick one out of the hat as the winner. But the draw isn't till next month, so I've got to keep the tickets safe until then. If they draw my ticket out of the hat, then I show them the other half of the ticket to prove I bought it! Don't you see?"

The budgie shook his head.

"The letter in Pauline's pocket said that Madge had to bring her winning raffle ticket to the store to receive her prize. That means she's probably got her part of the ticket in the house somewhere!"

"I get it! I get it!" cheeped Buddy, bobbing his head excitedly. "If we can find the ticket before

Pauline, she won't be able to get the prize!"

Joe sagged a bit. "But what if Pauline already has Madge's half of the ticket as well as the letter? And anyway, there's no way I can get inside the house to look!"

Buddy let out a long sad whistle. "We'll never stop Pauline!" Then he plucked out one of his feathers. "*One, two, buckle my shoe, three, four, knock at the door!*"

"Don't start saying all that silly stuff again!" said Joe. "And stop pulling out your feathers! You've already got a bald patch on your wing, you know!"

"*Five, six, pick up sticks, seven, eight, lay them straight!*"

PLUCK!
PLUCK!
PLUCK!

UNDEAD PETS

Joe sighed. It was probably best to leave him to it. He kicked off his shoes and pulled a pair of jeans out of his drawer. He couldn't wait to get out of the stinky "lost property" joggers!

"Joe! What's this?" Mum stood in the doorway holding the plastic bag stuffed with Joe's wet clothes. "I found it in your schoolbag!"

Joe's face reddened. "It's my trousers and my pants. I had a bit of an accident."

Mum gasped.

"No!" he said quickly. "I didn't wet myself! I sort of fell in a bucket of soapy water…"

"Oh, right," said Mum. "And how do you explain the lumps of kiwi fruit?"

"Well, er, it was soapy water mixed with fruit smoothie — kiwi fruit and lime smoothie."

Mum smiled. "Of course it was! Why didn't I think of that?" She rolled her eyes.

Nothing Joe did seemed to surprise his Mum any more. He'd been in so many scrapes lately that this sort of thing counted as pretty normal behaviour. And there was no way he could tell her that it was all thanks to the undead pets!

"When you're ready," Mum said, "would you come downstairs and help me sort out the leaflets? I've had another idea for a promotion, too!"

"Oh yeah? What's that?" Joe asked.

"I'm going to knock on a few doors when we're delivering the leaflets tomorrow and offer half-price, on-the-spot haircuts."

"What, on the doorstep?"

Mum nodded. "Well, not actually on the doorstep! Inside would do. What do you think?"

"Er…"

"Everyone loves a bargain, Joe!" said Mum.

"Everyone loves a bargain, Joe!" repeated Buddy. "B.O.G.O.F., Buddy! B.O.G.O.F. – Buy one, get one free! Look after the pennies and the pounds will look after themselves! Everyone loves a bargain, Joe."

Joe stared at Buddy. Of course! Madge was a total penny-pincher! She'd love a half-price haircut. All they had to do was turn up on her doorstep and offer it to her … then he'd be able to get into her house and look for the raffle ticket!

The only trouble was, he had no idea where she lived.

CHAPTER SIX

Joe scrolled down the page of addresses and phone numbers he'd found on the internet.

A. PRINGLE

A.A.R. PRINGLE

A.M. PRINGLE

C. PRINGLE

Rev D. PRINGLE

D.W. J. PRINGLE

Dr. G. PRINGLE

"Oh no!" he groaned. "There are seven M. Pringles listed! How am I supposed to knock on seven doors?" He glanced at the addresses. Half of the streets he'd never even heard of. "They're probably spread out all over town."

Buddy fluttered round Joe's head, then landed clumsily on his shoulder. He cocked his head and looked curiously at the computer.

"Do you recognize any of the addresses?" Joe nodded to the screen. But Buddy just shrugged. Then Joe remembered Buddy probably couldn't read. "What about this," Joe said, reading the first. "Number 11 Dover Sole Street?"

Buddy began whistling tunelessly to himself.

"47b Hartley Rise?"

Still nothing.

"Hang on," said Joe. "Pauline Pringle must be listed here as well. So if I can find a P. Pringle with the same address as an M. Pringle, then that's the one!"

Undead Pets

He glanced up and down the list. "There!" he said. "29 Argyll Avenue?"

Suddenly, Buddy squawked, "Buddy Pringle, 29 Argyll Avenue, telephone number 456773!"

"What?" Joe glanced up.

Buddy had hopped on to the shelf above the computer. "Buddy Pringle, 29 Argyll Avenue, telephone number 456773."

"Is that where you live?"

"Buddy Pringle, 29 Argyll Avenue, telephone number 456773."

"Buddy!" said Joe. "Snap out of it!" He clapped his hands.

Buddy jerked back to normal again.

"Did you live in Argyll Avenue?" asked Joe.

Buddy nodded. "Madge taught me to say my address in case I got lost."

Joe rolled his eyes. "Why didn't you say so? Bird brain!" He grinned. "Argyll Avenue's not far from here."

Buddy began bobbing his head up and down, flapping his wings and chirping. "Can we go? Can we go now?"

Joe shut down the computer. "Tomorrow, Buddy. We'll go tomorrow."

"Not fish fingers again!" wailed Sarah.

It was teatime. Joe was sitting at the table with Toby and his big sister, Sarah.

"Sorry," said Mum, who was peering at a

street map she'd printed off the computer. "I've been too busy to do a big shop this week. So we're eating up what's in the freezer."

"I don't mind," mumbled Toby, his cheeks stuffed with chips. "I love fish fingers and chips!"

Sarah scowled at him.

Mum picked up a fluorescent yellow marker pen and drew a large circle round their neighbourhood, then a line down the middle.

"Is that where we're delivering the leaflets?" asked Joe.

Mum nodded.

Joe pointed his fork at the section with Argyll Avenue in it. "Maybe you and me could do that bit, Mum. And Matt said he'd help, too."

"No way!" snapped Sarah. "I'm doing Argyll Avenue – that's where Gabriella lives."

Joe groaned. That's why he knew that street. Gabriella was Sarah's best friend. He'd been in the car when they'd dropped Sarah off for sleepovers at Gabriella's house.

"I'm sure Joe won't mind if you do Argyll Avenue," said Mum. "Will you, Joe?"

"Er, well…" Joe tried to think of a good reason to say no.

Buddy, who had been sitting on the lampshade above their heads, suddenly gave a shriek. He dive-bombed down towards the table, knocking a layer of dust off the lamp and landing with a thud in front of Joe's plate. "Argyll Avenue? Argyll Avenue! That's Madge's street. Tell her you're doing that one, Joe!"

Joe took a deep breath. "Mum, I have to do that street because I promised someone that I'd deliver a leaflet to their house."

"Who?" demanded Sarah. "Who do you know in Argyll Avenue?"

Joe racked his brains. Apart from Madge and Pauline Pringle, there was no one!

"Well," said Joe, playing for time. He was trying to think of someone in his class that Sarah wouldn't know…

"No one!" declared Sarah. "He's just saying he wants to do Gabriella's street to annoy me." She shot him an evil look.

"Miss Pringle from our school!" burst out Joe.

"Who?" asked Mum.

All eyes were on him now. Even Toby had stopped chewing and was peering at him.

"One of the dinner ladies from school," he mumbled. "I sort of told Miss Pringle about your new business—" he tried to ignore Sarah's scowl— "and I said I'd be putting a leaflet through her door. She was really keen on booking an appointment."

"So what?" snapped Sarah. "I'll do it. There's no reason why *you* have to do it!"

"But…" Joe stuttered. "But—"

"Come on!" snapped Sarah. "Why does it have to be you?"

Buddy made a strange hissing noise. He was staring at Sarah. "She's mean!" he said. Then he flew at her and pecked her nose.

"Ow!" Sarah squealed.

"What is it?" Mum looked at Joe. "Did you throw something at Sarah?"

"No!"

"Maybe it was the same as what bit you, Joe!" Toby said.

"What?" Mum looked worried. "When did you get bitten, Joe?"

"Just on the way home from school. It might have been a flea…"

"A flea?" Mum looked appalled.

Joe gulped. "Yeah. Maybe the clothes I borrowed from school had fleas?"

Mum gasped.

"Or maybe not," said Joe quickly.

UNDEAD PETS

"Mum! My nose!" wailed Sarah.

"Let me look." Mum leaned over the table. "Oh, it does look a bit red." She gave Joe a searching look. "Are you sure you didn't throw something at your sister?"

"Yes!"

Buddy was back on the lampshade again, swinging back and forth, knocking off more dust.

"Achoo!" sneezed Mum as a little cloud of dust cascaded down. "Achoo! Achoo! Achoo!"

"Mum!" snapped Sarah. "What about my nose!"

Achoo!

Mum rubbed her eyes. "It looks OK now, Sarah. Achoo!" Mum sneezed again. "Achoo! Achoo!"

"Tell Joe that I'm doing Argyll Avenue," said Sarah crossly.

Mum sighed. "How about we all do it," she said. Then she sneezed again!

"You've got to stop pecking people!" said Joe as he got ready for bed.

Buddy, who was sitting on a model aeroplane that hung from Joe's ceiling, shrugged. "That's what budgies do!"

"Not all of them!"

"She deserved it."

Joe couldn't argue with that.

"Night, Buddy," he said, climbing into bed. "And don't let the bed bugs bite." He grinned. As soon as tea was over Mum had taken away the "lost property" tracksuit bottoms and put them straight in the washing machine – just in case they really had got fleas.

Joe closed his eyes.

"Twinkle, twinkle, little star…"

Joe groaned.

"How I wonder what you are…"

"Buddy!"

"Up above the world so high…"

"Stop it! I can't sleep with you twittering on."

"Baa, baa, black sheep—"

"BUDDY!" Joe flicked on the light.

"Sorry, Joe, but Madge and I always sang songs together before she put the cover over my cage." He looked around anxiously. "I don't think I can sleep with so much space around me."

"But I don't have a budgie cage," Joe said. At this rate he wouldn't get a wink of sleep. "Wait a minute." Joe climbed out of bed and crossed over to the cupboard. He rifled through piles of puzzles and games. "There!" He pulled out a large junk model made of old shoeboxes, yoghurt pots and scraps of paper.

"What is it?" asked Buddy uncertainly.

"It's a model T rex. I made it when I was six.

I got a prize for it at school!"

Buddy looked at the creature curiously.

"There you go," Joe said, putting it on top of his

chest of drawers. "It's a bit like a budgie cage."

Buddy flew into the dinosaur's mouth and peeped out. "I can still see the room!"

Joe sighed. Then he grabbed his T-shirt and draped it over the model. "Goodnight, Buddy."

There was no reply.

CHAPTER SEVEN

"Are you really going to knock on their door?" Matt still couldn't believe they were at the Pringle sisters' house.

It was Saturday morning, and they'd been delivering leaflets since eight o'clock. Argyll Avenue was their last street before a break.

Sarah, who was doing Gabriella's side of the street with Toby and Dad, stuck her tongue out at Joe. "Bet I get a customer before you!"

Joe made a face back at her. "Come on," he said to Matt.

UNDEAD PETS

Mum, who was handing over a leaflet to the lady who lived in the house next door to the Pringles, gave Joe a hopeful thumbs up. Lots of people were interested in booking appointments, but no one had wanted an instant haircut yet!

Joe rang the bell, his heart racing. Somehow he had to convince Madge to have her hair cut. And – most importantly – let him inside!

Buddy was sitting on Joe's shoulder twittering nervously. "Who's a pretty boy? Buddy boy! Buddy boy! Kissy, kissy!"

Just then the door opened. It was Madge Pringle.

"Yes? What is it?" She frowned at Joe and Matt.

"MADGE!" squawked Buddy with delight, fluttering over to sit on her shoulder, even though she had no idea he was there.

Joe smiled politely. Madge was wearing a bright orange cardigan, purple trousers and strange bottle-green fluffy slippers. Her wispy hair was wafting around in the breeze. She stared at Joe for a moment, trying to place him.

"Hello, Miss Pringle. It's Joe Edmunds, from school…"

"Yes? What do you want?"

Joe suddenly felt a bit tongue-tied.

"Would you like a half-price haircut?" blurted out Matt. "Right now!"

"What?" Madge looked at him as though he was mad. "You want to cut my hair?"

Joe tried not to laugh. "No! Not us — my mum." He handed her a leaflet. "She's a mobile hairdresser and she's offering a special deal today – a doorstep discount."

"A discount, you say?" Madge peered at the leaflet.

"Yeah, it's a special deal. Half-price haircuts if you get it done now!"

Madge looked a bit shocked. "What? Right now?"

Joe nodded. "That's my mum over there." He waved over to her and she came to join them.

"Good morning!" she smiled. "I'm Helen Edmunds. I run a mobile hairdressing business – I used to be the senior stylist at Cut Above."

Madge nodded. "Oh yes, my sister goes there. It's expensive, though, isn't it?"

Joe glanced at Madge's wild hair. It looked like she cut it herself – with garden shears!

"We're just handing out a few leaflets," said Joe's mum. "It's half price if you have your hair cut now. It's a special introductory offer."

UNDEAD PETS

"I see," said Madge. "Well, it sounds like a good deal." Madge inspected the price list printed on the leaflet and then smiled at Joe's mum. "Count me in!"

Mum beamed. "Great! I'll get my things from the car." She headed off before Madge could change her mind, leaving Joe and Matt on the doorstep.

"I suppose you two will want to come in for some juice while your mum's cutting my hair?"

"No!" squeaked Matt. "We've got more leaflets—"

Joe cut him off. "Thanks, Miss Pringle. That would be great!"

Matt frowned at Joe, but didn't say anything.

"What's going on?" Pauline Pringle had appeared in the hall.

"I'm having my hair cut!" said Madge. "I'll just get a towel. I said I'd give the boys some juice. Would you mind, Pauline?"

Pauline pursed her lips and peered at Joe. "*You* again!"

"Hello, Miss Pringle," said Joe nervously.

"His mum's going to give me a haircut," called Madge as she headed upstairs.

Pauline looked puzzled. "Now?"

"You could have one, too," Matt suggested, handing her a leaflet.

"Don't be cheeky!" she muttered. "Go on through." She nodded towards the living room.

Buddy was already waiting for them. He had flown straight through the wall and was now flapping around the room in big loops. "Look for the raffle ticket, Joe! It must be here somewhere!"

But Joe wasn't sure where to start. The room was full of stuff! There were two flowery sofas, an old armchair and loads of shelves and cupboards with ornaments inside.

Matt made a face. "Yuck!" he whispered.

"Look at all this stuff — it's gross!"

"Madge is very proud of her china," squawked Buddy, fluttering crossly round Matt's head. "What does he know?"

An old-fashioned clock in the centre of the mantelpiece chimed the half hour. Joe jumped.

"Don't touch anything!" said Pauline, coming in carrying a tray with two small glasses of juice on it. "Sit down, and sit still!"

Joe's mum appeared with her bag of equipment. "Where shall I set up? Most people find that the kitchen's best."

Pauline nodded. "Follow me!"

"Find the raffle ticket!" squawked Buddy.

"Do you think you should be touching that?" asked Matt as Joe started picking up the ornaments and looking at them.

Joe reached for a small china ballerina.

"Stop!" hissed Matt. "Pauline'll go crazy if she sees you!"

UNDEAD PETS

Joe shrugged. "I was just wondering if they were … antiques."

"Since when did you become an expert?"

"Dad likes watching antique shows," said Joe, picking up another ornament and pretending to look at the markings on the bottom of it.

"Over here, Joe!" squawked Buddy.

He was fluttering round a bookcase in the corner of the room. On the top was a large vase with flowers painted on it.

"I can see something inside!" cried Buddy.

Joe grabbed a chair and pushed it over to the bookcase.

"What are you doing?" gasped Matt.

"Just checking… I think that's a very rare vase."

"What are you on about?"

Joe was standing on the chair now, his hands on the vase, when suddenly Pauline appeared in the doorway.

"HEY!" she yelled.

Joe jumped in fright and lost his balance. He grabbed the bookcase to steady himself and it wobbled violently. Joe managed to stop himself from falling, but the vase shook, then fell forward. He tried to catch it, but it slipped through his fingers and crashed to the ground.

Pauline's mouth opened, but no words came out. Joe looked at the vase in horror. It lay on the floor in pieces.

"What was that noise?" called Madge from the kitchen.

"The boy broke one of your vases!" Pauline yelled back.

"Joe!" said Mum, appearing behind Pauline, her scissors still in her hand.

"I can explain," said Joe in a small voice.

"He thought the vase was antique," said Matt, trying to help.

Joe looked at his shoes. "I'm really sorry…"

"I'll expect my haircut for free now!" yelled Madge from the kitchen.

CHAPTER EIGHT

"It was there, I saw it!" shrieked Buddy. He was sitting on Joe's shoulder as they walked back to the car. "The raffle ticket was lying in the broken bits of vase!"

Joe nodded. He'd seen it, too. And so had Pauline. She'd put it in her pocket when she thought no one was looking. But there was nothing Joe could do about it now. Mum had sent him and Matt to wait in the car.

"I told you not to touch anything," grumbled Matt.

Joe nodded miserably.

"Do you think your mum will still pay us?" asked Matt.

"I doubt it," he said. But getting paid for delivering Mum's leaflets was the least of his worries!

"What are we going to do now?" wailed Buddy.

Joe shrugged. Even if he had a plan, which he didn't, it wasn't as if he could discuss it now – not in front of Matt.

Buddy tucked his head under his wing and began babbling, *"Pat a cake, pat a cake, baker's man, bake me a cake as fast as you can!"*

"How could you?" said Mum, getting into the driver's seat and slamming the car door behind her. "Not only did I have to do the cut for free, but I'm sure Madge Pringle will tell all her neighbours what happened. I'll never work in this street again!"

"Sorry, Mum."

"Sorry, Mum, sorry, Mum! Silly billy, Joe!" Buddy chirped.

Joe wished Buddy would put a sock in it!

"You know you shouldn't touch other people's property!" said Mum.

"Maybe you could buy her another vase," suggested Matt. "There's that sale on at Beddows tomorrow – they've got loads of horrible vases."

Mum scowled. "Thanks, Matt, but I don't think that will help."

Joe sat up straight. Actually, making sure he was at Beddows at the same time as Pauline Pringle might not be a bad thing. Perhaps there was still a chance he could stop her claiming the raffle prize. He wasn't sure how, but if he could come up with something…

"Please could I buy Miss Pringle something else," pleaded Joe. "I've still got some of my birthday money left. I'd like to get her something to make up for the vase."

Mum sighed. "It's a nice idea, Joe, but—"

Just then there was a knock on Mum's car window. It was Sarah.

"Gabriella's mum says she'd like a haircut!" she said, smiling proudly. "In fact, her whole family wants one!"

Joe made a face.

"Well done, Sarah!" Mum beamed.

"Guess I got more customers than you, Joe. I win!"

Joe didn't say anything. He was hoping Mum wouldn't tell Sarah about the vase. If she did, he'd never hear the end of it.

"What's the plan?" asked Buddy. He was perched on the mirror as Joe brushed his teeth.

"Dunno." Joe spat out a mouthful of toothpaste. He'd been trying to come up with a new plan all day, but he hadn't got anywhere.

"Dunno? Dunno?" repeated Buddy. Then he caught sight of himself in the mirror and pecked his reflection. "Who's a pretty boy then? Beautiful Buddy!"

Joe put his toothbrush back in the pot. "Maybe I could just wait until Pauline's about to get her prize, and then shout out something about it being the wrong sister."

Buddy cocked his head to one side. "Would that work?"

"Doubt it! I'd probably get into even more trouble with Mum, too."

"Why can't you just tell Madge she's the winner?"

Joe wiped his mouth on the towel. "Because she'd want to know how I found out!" He sighed. "I can hardly tell her that her undead budgie told me! If only someone else could tell her — like the manager of the department store." He froze. "Maybe he could!"

"What?" Buddy blinked at him. "How?"

"Well, it wouldn't actually be the manager. It would be me! I could pretend to be calling from the store to tell her she's the winner!"

Buddy gave a shriek. "Great plan, Joe!"

"There's one problem. I don't sound like a grown-up. My voice isn't deep enough." Joe frowned. "Unless I could change my voice somehow."

"How?"

"I know! Follow me!" Joe raced out of the bathroom and down the hall to Toby's room. He pushed the door open slowly…

A light immediately went out and Toby dived back into bed, burrowing under the covers.

"It's all right, it's me!" Joe said.

Toby peeped out. "Oh, hi, Joe!"

Joe flicked on the light. Lego was scattered across the floor.

"I wanted to finish building the rocket!" whispered Toby. "Don't tell!"

"I won't," said Joe. "If you let me borrow your voice changer."

"My what?"

"That thing you got for Christmas," Joe pulled open one of Toby's drawers and began rummaging through it. "It was blue, and when you talked into it, it made your voice sound different."

UNDEAD PETS

"I remember!" squeaked Toby. He jumped out of bed and pulled open another drawer.

Buddy perched on the curtain rail, while the boys searched through Toby's stuff.

"Wow!" Toby said, finding a light-up yo-yo at the back of the drawer. "Look, Joe!"

"Great! But where's the voice changer?" Joe pulled open another drawer.

"HELLO, JOE!" said a robotic voice.

He spun round. Toby was grinning at him, with the voice changer in his hand.

"I found it!" Toby said proudly.

"Let me see." Joe examined the toy. There were four settings: Low, high, alien and robot. "Stand Back, Earthling!" Joe said, on the alien setting.

Toby giggled.

"Exterminate!" Joe zapped Toby with an imaginary ray gun.

"Ahh!" Toby shrieked and dropped to the floor, jerking for a few seconds, then lying still.

"What's going on in here?" Dad stood in the doorway. He looked at Toby, then at the mess of Lego. "Have you been out of bed with your torch again, Toby?"

"Sorry. It's my fault," said Joe. "I just came in to borrow something and woke him up."

Dad frowned. "Mmm, right!" He smiled. "Go on then! Back to bed, both of you!"

Joe raced to his room before Dad could ask any more questions!

CHAPTER NINE

"Tell me the plan again," Buddy twittered.

It was Sunday morning and Joe was in the hall, lacing up his trainers. Buddy was perched on his shoulder.

"We're going to sneak round to Madge's house," Joe replied.

"Uh-huh!" said Buddy.

"Then we hide and keep watch until Pauline leaves for the shops…"

"Uh-huh!" Buddy gave another enormous nod and nearly fell off Joe's shoulder.

"Then I call Madge – you gave me the number, remember…"

"Buddy Pringle, 29 Argyll Avenue, telephone number 456773."

"Yeah, that's it!" said Joe.

"Buddy Pringle, 29 Argyll Avenue, telephone number 456773."

"Yeah, I got it, Buddy!"

"Buddy Pringle, 29 Argyll A—"

"Stop!" said Joe, and he clapped his hands.

Buddy gave himself a shake. "Sorry."

"Then I'll use the voice changer to pretend to be the manager calling from the store. I'll tell Madge that she's won the raffle prize and that she has to come and collect it!"

"Great plan, Joe!"

"Yeah," Joe stood up, "it is. But first I have to get my hands on a mobile phone."

Joe wasn't allowed a mobile until he went to secondary school, the same as Sarah.

UNDEAD PETS

"Of course!" Joe said suddenly. "I'll borrow Sarah's!" He could hear the shower going. "Her phone will be in her room," he said. "Come on!"

He sneaked past the bathroom, down the hall and into Sarah's room.

Joe held his nose. Sarah liked really stinky perfume. The room was cluttered with make-up and hair products, and the walls were covered in vampire film posters. Joe felt his heart pounding. He was never – NOT EVER! – allowed in Sarah's room. If he got caught she'd go ballistic.

He spotted Sarah's phone on her bedside table. As he reached for it, it beeped. Joe jumped. But it was just a text message.

Buddy was twittering nervously above Joe's head, swinging back and forth on Sarah's purple lampshade.

Joe pocketed the phone and crept out of the room as quickly as he could. Then he grabbed the voice changer from his room and bounded down the stairs.

"Back in a bit, Mum!" he yelled. "Just got to take something to Matt!"

He banged the door behind him, jumped on his bike and set off with Buddy still clinging to his shoulder, digging his claws in.

As he skidded to a halt two doors away from Madge's house, Joe glanced at his watch. "Ten o'clock," he said. "We've got two hours before the presentation in the store. Hopefully Pauline will head off to the shops early."

"Pauline loves shopping," cheeped Buddy. "Naughty Pauline shops till she drops!"

As he spoke, the Pringles' front door opened and Pauline appeared.

"Duck!" Joe yelled. Then he remembered that no one apart from him could actually see Buddy. It was only him that needed to hide! He dropped down behind a parked car. "Did she see me?" he whispered.

Buddy fluttered up to take a look. "Nope! She's gone off the other way."

"Good! We can call Madge." Joe took out Sarah's mobile phone and the voice changer. "Buddy, tell me your phone number again."

"Buddy Pringle, 29 Argyll Avenue, telephone number 456773."

Joe tapped in the numbers. There was a pause, then it started to ring. Joe set the phone to loud speaker.

"Hello?" Madge said. "Who is it?"

UNDEAD PETS

Joe took a deep breath, then put the voice changer to his lips. "HELLO?" he said. Except he'd pressed the wrong button and instead of "low" he'd set it to "alien"!

"Who is this?" Madge snapped. "What's going on?"

Joe quickly changed the setting on the voice changer, but his hands were shaking now.

"Sorry about that," he said through the voice changer. The low setting sounded better than alien, but still a bit strange.

"Who is it?" demanded Madge again.

Joe cleared his throat. "Hello, I'm calling from Beddows Department Store."

"What?"

"BEDDOWS DEPARTMENT STORE!" boomed Joe.

"Oh yes?" Madge sounded slightly friendlier.

"You've won our raffle!"

"What?"

"Congratulations!"

"I've won?" Madge sounded shocked.

Joe swallowed again. "Yes ... and you need to collect your prize from our store today at twelve noon."

There was a pause.

Joe crossed his fingers. What if she didn't believe him? What if she still thought it was a prank.

"Your voice sounds a bit odd," said Madge suspiciously.

"The phone isn't working very well!" Joe replied.

"Oh," said Madge. There was another pause.

"And I've really won the prize?"

"We sent you a letter," said Joe.

"What letter? I didn't get a letter."

Joe thought he'd better hang up now. "Not to worry, see you at midday. Goodbye." He quickly ended the call. Buddy was fluttering around him nervously. "Do you think she believed me?"

"I'll go and see!"

"But how can you get in?" called Joe. Then he remembered — Buddy was an undead pet. He didn't need an invitation! Joe watched him fly straight through the wall of the house.

The phone beeped. It was another text message. He wondered how crazy his sister was going right now, looking for her lost phone.

In a blink Buddy was back. "Madge is putting her coat on!"

"Really?" Joe grinned at the budgie. "She believed me then?"

Buddy nodded. "And she went looking

for her raffle ticket. I don't think she could remember where she'd put it, then she spotted the gap where the vase that you broke used to be and suddenly she looked a bit cross. I heard her say 'Pauline!' in an angry voice."

"Do you think she suspects Pauline of pinching it?"

Buddy shrugged.

Just then they heard the Pringles' door opening again. Joe ducked behind the car. "What's happening?" he hissed.

Buddy fluttered up to look. "Madge is locking the front door. She's going the same way Pauline went!"

"We did it!" Joe whispered. He punched the air victoriously.

"JOE EDMUNDS! What are you doing here?" said a horribly familiar voice.

Joe gasped. It was Gabriella. She stood glowering at Joe, tossing her blonde curls and twisting her mouth into a nasty sneer.

"I…" Joe felt his face turn beetroot. "I was finishing off delivering the leaflets for Mum, but I fell off my bike."

Gabriella's eyes narrowed. "I thought Sarah delivered the rest of the leaflets."

Joe climbed back on to his bike without answering. "Got to go!" he said.

"Tell Sarah I've been texting her," yelled Gabriella.

Joe pedalled away as fast as he could.

CHAPTER TEN

"Where have you been, Joe?" Mum was waiting for him in the hall, tapping her watch. "We're supposed to be going shopping this morning, remember!"

"Well, I'm not going anywhere until I find my phone," bellowed Sarah from the living room.

Joe felt his cheeks burning. The phone was in his pocket. "Does she have to come?" he whispered to Mum.

"Sarah needs new school shoes. I might as well get them in the sale."

UNDEAD PETS

"Where is it?" he heard Sarah shriek. She was thundering round the house like an angry elephant, turning everything upside down.

"Mum!" yelled Toby. "Sarah just shoved me off the sofa!"

"I'm checking down the side of the cushions!" she shouted. "Joe? Where's Joe? I bet he pinched it!"

Joe tiptoed upstairs.

"You can't just accuse your brother," he heard Mum say. "You need to take more care of your possessions, Sarah!"

Joe ran the rest of the way, straight into the bathroom. He shut the door, then took out the phone and put it down next to Sarah's toothbrush.

"What are you doing?" asked Buddy, who'd appeared through the wall.

"Just watch," he said. "SARAH!" he yelled.

"WHAT?"

"I just found your phone in the bathroom!"

There was a pause. "But I didn't leave it there!"

They got to the department store just before twelve.

"I'm going to look at the clothes," said Sarah sulkily.

"No, let's go to the shoe department first," said Mum.

"Joe!" squawked Buddy suddenly. "There's Pauline!"

She was on the escalator, heading upstairs.

"Quick!" said Buddy. "We need to follow her."

Joe glanced around. Madge should be there by now, too. He looked at his watch – only a couple of minutes to go until the prizegiving.

"Dad?" said Joe.

"Mmmm?"

UNDEAD PETS

"Fancy some free cake?"

Joe pointed to a large sign nearby:

RAFFLE PRIZEGIVING!
Free cake in Beddows Café
First floor at 12 p.m.

Toby's eyes lit up.

Joe headed for the escalator and Buddy flew off ahead. Toby ran to follow.

"Slow down, Joe!" called Dad. "No! Toby! Stay with me!"

His little brother stopped and waited for Dad, but Joe pretended he hadn't heard. He took off up the moving steps, dodging past other shoppers.

"Careful!" called an old man.

"Sorry, sorry!" called Joe as he passed the other people.

"Over there!" squawked Buddy.

Joe jumped off the top step of the escalator and dashed over to the café, where a man in a smart suit was standing next to a photographer. A crowd of customers was waiting in front of them. Joe could see Pauline in the middle. But there was no sign of Madge.

"Thank you so much for coming to Beddows today," the man in the suit said, "and for helping us to celebrate fifty years of business. As a special thank you to all our loyal customers we'll be serving cake in a moment. But first we'd like to present our grand raffle prize – a gift voucher to the value of five hundred pounds to spend in store."

There was a round of applause. Joe could see Pauline straightening her coat, getting ready to go up and claim the prize.

UNDEAD PETS

"Where's Madge?" shrieked Buddy. He was fluttering around the group. "I can't see Madge!"

"And the winner of the grand prize draw is … Miss Madge Pringle!"

"That's me!" said Pauline, waving Madge's raffle ticket in the air. "I'm Madge Pringle!"

"No, you're not!" shrieked Buddy helplessly. He fluttered towards Pauline as though he was about to peck her nose!

But just then another voice repeated what Buddy had said.

"NO, YOU'RE NOT!" Joe spun round to see who was speaking. "I'm Madge Pringle!"

The real Madge Pringle was standing at the top of the escalator. Her hair was messed up and her cheeks were red. She looked like she'd been running.

A look of horror passed over Pauline's face. Her mouth dropped open. "I… I…" she muttered.

The customers looked from Pauline to Madge, then back again.

The store manager looked at the photographer, then at Madge and Pauline. "Who is Madge Pringle?" he asked the two sisters.

"*She* is!" Joe heard himself shout, pointing to Madge. "The lady with the frizzy hair!"

He clamped his hand over his mouth. He hadn't meant to sound rude.

But Madge smiled at him and marched forward. "I'm Madge Pringle. I got held up – my bus broke down. That woman is my sister!"

"Is that true?" asked the manager. He didn't look like he wanted to argue with Madge.

"Yes," said Pauline in a small voice. "I thought I should pick up Madge's prize for her, because I … didn't think she was going to be here today!"

Madge's face was thunderous. "Really!" she said. "Well, that's probably because I didn't get the letter they sent me!"

Pauline gulped. Her face turned from white to crimson.

"Thank goodness you called me," said Madge, smiling at the store manager.

He looked puzzled. "But, I didn't—"

"Can we have a picture of Madge with her prize, please?" said the photographer.

Joe gave a sigh of relief.

A waitress appeared pushing a large trolley of cake.

"Don't mind if I do," said Dad, who'd appeared with Toby, as he took a slice of cake from the waitress. He turned to Joe. "You shouldn't have run off like that. I had to find Mum and Sarah to tell them where we were going!"

"Sorry, Dad." Joe took a slice of cake.

"We did it!" cheeped Buddy, landing on Joe's shoulder, his chest puffed up with pride. "We saved Madge's money!"

"Do you think she'll forgive Pauline for stealing her letter?" Joe whispered.

Buddy shrugged. "Sisters! Can't live with 'em, can't live without 'em!"

Joe giggled.

Just then, Sarah appeared. She marched up to the cake trolley and helped herself to the largest slice.

"Bye, Joe," chirped Buddy. "Thanks for everything."

Joe looked around, but Buddy had already vanished. A small green feather fluttered down. Joe caught it and held it on his palm.

"Hello, Joe!" It was Madge Pringle. "Thanks for speaking up for me just now."

"That's OK." Joe looked at his feet, hoping that Miss Pringle wasn't going to tell him off for saying she had frizzy hair.

But she didn't. "Doing some shopping, are you?" she asked.

"I was going to get you another vase," said Joe.

"Don't worry about that. I can buy plenty of vases now — I just won the raffle!"

Pauline sidled past, looking miserable.

"I might even treat my sister to something!" said Madge in a loud voice.

Pauline's face lit up. "Really?"

"I've seen some lovely china budgies," Madge added. "I thought we could buy a matching pair to remind us of Buddy!"

Pauline groaned and Joe giggled.

Gifts and
China ⇨